Have You Considered Murder?

LIANA BROOKS

OTHER WORKS

ALL I WANT FOR CHRISTMAS

All I Want For Christmas Is A Reaper
All I Want For Christmas Is A Werewolf

FLEET OF MALIK

Bodies In Motion
Change of Momentum

HEROES AND VILLAINS

Even Villains Fall In Love
Even Villains Go To The Movies
Even Villains Have Interns
Even Villains Play The Hero (omnibus)
The Polar Terror

TIME AND SHADOWS
The Day Before
Convergence Point
Decoherence

SHORTER WORKS

Fey Lights
Prime Sensations
Darkness and Good

Find other works by the author at
www.lianabrooks.com

Have You Considered Murder?

INKLET #49

LIANA BROOKS

www.inkprintpress.com

Print ISBN: 978-1-925825-51-0
eBook ISBN: 9781393870869

www.inkprintpress.com

National Library of Australia Cataloguing-in-Publication Data
Brooks, Liana 1982 –
Have You Considered Murder?
42 p.
ISBN: 978-1-925825-51-0
Inkprint Press, Canberra, Australia
1. Fiction—Crime 2. Fiction—Humorous—General 3. Fiction—Short Stories

First Print Edition: January 2021
Cover photo © donterase via Pixabay
Cover design © Inkprint Press
Interior art © Amy Laurens

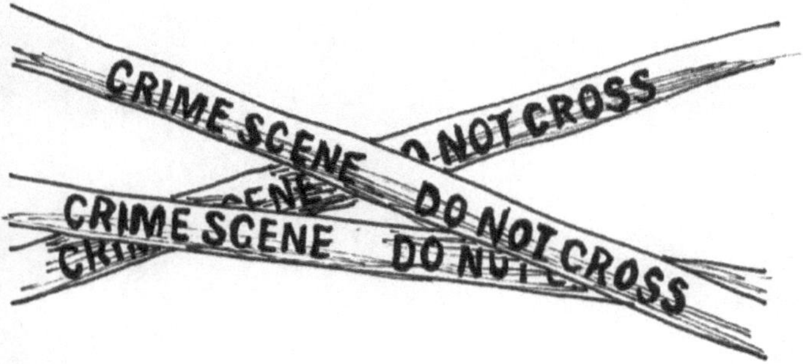

CRIME SCENE   DO NOT CROSS

CRIME SCENE   DO NOT CROSS

HAVE YOU CONSIDERED MURDER?

"**H**AVE YOU CONSIDERED MURDER?"

The words floated between the steam of the subways and the smell of rotting food in the dumpster like a pick-up line from the devil. Street-lights flickered fitfully in the dark.

Jack turned and stared at the witness, her brown hair in a messy bun and the oversized NYU hoodie hanging to the ground as she knelt in the dimly-lit alleyway.

She looked up with big, dark eyes. "Murder is always an option."

"What?" Jack demanded.

"How..." Rob waved a hand at the witness and the duct tape hanging limp from her mouth.

How was a good question. She was supposed to be tied up.

The girl shrugged her shoulder, her sweatshirt flopping up and down. "The knock-off duct tape really isn't strong enough. Really, you need to use the patented brand. But, that's off topic. Look, the solution here is murder."

"Murder?" Jack frowned.

"You have a gun," the witness said. "Just shoot me! Quick! Clean! I don't have to worry about you hunting me down. It saves me time and anxiety. You don't have to worry about me going to the police." She let the thought dangle.

Jack and Rob exchanged glances. "I mean..."

"Of course you have a new worry. One of you will be a murderer and the other will be a witness. That sort of thing can break a friendship. But it definitely won't be my problem. So. Bang bang. Dead? Right? Can we get on with it? Kneeling really isn't comfortable."

Jack shook his head. "Wait. You want to die?"

"Want is a strong word," the girl said. "But it's better than the alternative, right?"

"What *is* the alternative?" Rob asked, frowning in burgeoning confusion.

The witness sighed, her expression pitiful and sad. "It's something terrible. I don't want to burden you."

"Cancer?" Jack asked. That would make sense. Someone with only a few weeks left to live might pick a bullet over palliative care.

"Chronic disease? Disability?" Rob asked.

The girl looked at them like they were fleas she'd found in her water glass. "Ew! Excuse me! That's super abelist. Are you saying people with disabilities can't live full and rewarding lives? Wow. Just... *Wow!* I mean, robbing a bank I understand, but this." She shook her head." You really are trash. No. Thank you. I'm perfectly healthy and enlightened enough that I know not to trash other people's lives or assume the worst."

Jack rolled his eyes. "We're just trying to figure out why you want to die."

"Student loans?" Rob guessed, oblivious to the insults.

"I had scholarships, actually," the witness said. "And my life is perfectly sanguine."

"I don't know what that word means," Rob said.

"Fine," Jack and the witness said together.

Jack raised the hand with the gun. "Listen, why do you want to die?"

"Because it's convenient?" The girl glared at him like he was an idiot.

Which, fair enough, he was standing outside the place he'd broken into without setting off an alarm and arguing with the witness. Maybe he *was* an idiot. "Murder doesn't look good on a rap sheet."

"Neither does breaking and entering or theft," the girl said. "I figured if you were willing to break that law, then murder would be fine too."

"Yeah, but, why?" He shook his head again. "What could be worse than death?"

The girl pursed her lips together then grimaced in the over-exaggerated way of aspiring Broadway actresses everywhere. "Well, just hypothetically here, if you were the oldest granddaughter who happened to have— *maybe*—lied to the family about a long-term boyfriend and you were—and this is just *hypothetical* of course—supposed to be bringing the man to your youngest cousin's wedding in two weeks and you didn't actually *have* said man in your life…" She tilted her head. "Then… Maybe… Hear me out here… Maybe being murdered would make your family less angry."

Rob shook his head. "No. That's a terrible idea. You'll ruin the wedding!"

"You say ruin. I say upstage. Everyone will say they loved me." The girl nodded enthusiastically.

"What you need to do is find a gay guyfriend and have him go with you," Rob said.

"What? Is this a 90's romcom? Am I Julia Roberts? No. It's never going to happen." She paused to inhale, then shook her head. "It wouldn't work. Three of my cousins are lesbians and they'd notice in a minute. I can't fake eighteen months of romance with a guy like that. They'd know something was up. Dead is better. Can you, like, aim for my heart? I'd like an open-casket funeral."

Jack tucked the gun into the waistband of his pants. "We're not killing you!"

"What!" The witness's voice echoed in the still night air. "Why not?! I thought we had an agreement! You were going to help me out here!"

"Not by killing you!" Jack said.

"Are *you* free next Saturday?" the girl asked hopefully.

"No!" Jack blinked. "I'm in a relationship."

Rob raised his hand. "Very gay. Sorry."

"Don't ever apologize for being yourself," the witness said. She stood up, shaking off the ropes.

Jack's mouth moved soundlessly.

The witness looked down at the bindings. "You really, really need to use the good stuff. This rope has too much stretch. It's like being tied up by bungee cords. I mean, no judgement if that's your kink, but it's *not* a great way to get someone to hold still. My knees are killing me. So... murder or no murder?"

"No murder!" Jack shouted. "We don't even know you that well!"

"True," Rob chimed in.

"Oh, true." The witness nodded. "Most women are murdered by someone they know. Ex-lovers, domestic partners, that sort of thing. I'm Lindsey, by the by."

"Rob," Rob said with a friendly smile. "This is Jack!"

Jack nearly had a heart attack. "*Why* are you *saying* anything? We're not friends!"

"Not with that attitude," Rob said.

"Jack sounds like a good ex-boyfriend name," Lindsey said.

Jack closed his eyes. Somehow the

night had gotten away from him. "Okay. No. We're not dating."

"Obviously!" Lindsey said, folding her arms. "You two-timing bastard."

"And we are not killing anyone!" Jack glared at her.

Rob's shoulders slumped. "Fine. Man. I'm bummed."

"Why?" Jack demanded.

"I thought you two were good together," Rob said. "You had real chemistry."

Maybe he'd hit his head coming out of the building.

Maybe he'd died.

Maybe he was high... That made sense. Contact high from something. He was tripping. It was probably Rob's fault.

A broken bottle rolled across the alley as someone walked in. "Hey, guys?"

"Steve!" Rob waved.

"What is taking so long?" the getaway driver asked.

Jack waved a hand at the girl. "We just ran into…"

"… Jack's ex," Rob said. "They were trying to get back together but it's not working."

"Hey, not cool," Steve said. "Leave your love life at home, Romeo. This is work." He held out a hand. "Hi, Steve. You are…?"

"Lindsey." She shook his hand. "It's okay. We were really just talking because I need a date for my cousin's wedding next weekend and Jack's being unreasonable."

Steve shook his head. "That is so like him. Always busy with work. Planning this. Grifting that. It's unending."

"He's obsessed with work," Lindsey said, peeling away the last of the duct tape and balling it up. "All I wanted was a date for next Saturday."

"He could have made the time," Steve said.

Lindsey tilted her head and smiled. "What are you doing next weekend?"

"Nothing… yet." Steve smiled.

Jack blinked as their getaway driver walked away with their witness.

From the end of the alley he heard Steve ask Lindsey what she did for a living. "Nothing exciting really," was the answer. "But I was just promoted to detective…"

THE MAKING OF *HAVE YOU CONSIDERED MURDER?*

Well... have you? Have you ever considered murder as a way to avoid your problems?

I have.

It's part of my job, really. I write murder on an almost daily basis. In fiction, there's less chance of murder resulting in life in prison. So let's keep it to fiction. Or leave it for those instances where you really need to confuse your enemies.

Read more by Liana Brooks!

ALL I WANT FOR CHRISTMAS IS A WEREWOLF

THERE WAS MISTLETOE OVER MY DESK. Honest to goodness mistletoe hanging over the remains of my Halloween festivities. The Great Pumpkin was now overshadowed by a hemiparasitic shrub.

When I'd left for a conference two hours ago, my desk had been a bastion against the winter holidays. A snow-free island in an otherwise elegantly decorated office suite dedicated to art.

The gallery's front foyer with the dark wood paneling and over-stuffed pine-green tub chairs was now displaying glass and metal snowflakes in dazzling designs.

The main negotiating room, with the long table suitable for a fleet of lawyers, had a festive Seasons Greetings banner with pine trees and bright red birds signed by various Miami athletes.

The hall had garlands, multi-colored lights, and occasionally holiday music blaring out of incautiously opened offices.

But this?

This monstrous greenery was not supposed to touch my space.

Elegant Miami's main art gallery across the MacArthur Causeway was a glittering gem of holiday art. But over here, at the offices on Miami Beach that had been selected specifically to be near my boss's favorite house, things were toned down.

This was where Elegant Miami hid the nitty gritty details of business. It was the safe space for the sales people that spent all day on the phone with overseas clients; it was the home base of the style teams who went and decorated Miami palaces with carefully curated art from around the world; it was a soulless sovereignty of the contracts office where Maureen and I made sure every jot and tittle were in place.

Tittle was one of my co-worker's favorite words. It means the dot over a lower case I or J, but it sounds funny. Stuck in an L-shaped, linoleum-floored concrete bunker with two high windows that looked at the neighboring building a foot away and that always smelled of nail polish and mildew, we took our fun where we could find it.

But I drew the line at plastic Naughty Santa window clings blocking the little sunlight available. Being held hostage by forced holiday cheer was not part of my paycheck.

"Happy holidays, Del!" Maureen jumped out from behind my desk wearing a bright blue sweater with silver bells, dancing elves, and snowflakes. The bell at the end of her bright pink

Santa hat with pole dancing elves jingled as she stilled.

I stared, carefully counting to ten in every language I could remember, willing the other half the contracts team to vanish. It wasn't enough. Maureen and her seasonal cheer remained where they were.

"Don't you love it? I'm going to spray some fake snow too!" She pointed around at the sad, red tinsel garlands hanging off the black filing cabinets and the tiny palm tree that was sagging under a strand of rainbow lights.

"That's really not necessary," I said carefully circling around the hazardous airspace of the parasitic plant of unwanted kisses.

What was Maureen even thinking? Who on earth was I going to kiss here? It was against my personal policy to kiss clients or married people. That left Rafael Kane, office grinch, as the only possible target of unwanted contact.

Granted, he was a hot and sexy Office Grinch, but he was also the person voted most likely to ruin a party. He didn't chitchat. He didn't get distracted. He didn't waste time talking to coworkers, going to long Friday lunches, or building friendships.

Rafael Kane went to work, smiled for his clients only, and made Elegant Miami over fifteen percent of our yearly profit. We all loved him for his sales acumen, and stunning good looks, but no one around here considered him a friend.

Very early on, I'd tried. But Rafael Kane had taken one look at me, snarled like I'd stabbed his grandma, and avoided me ever since.

Which suited me just fine.

I frowned. If Maureen thought there was any chance of an office romance, my desk would look like an ad for the Great Bridal Expo. I needed tiny white seed pearls and chiffon as much as I needed mistletoe, which was about as much as a shark needed a tuba.

My idea of a good date was streaming a good murder mystery. I liked crime shows, creepy horror movies, and all things Halloween. People joked that I was a pagan, but that wasn't exactly true. I just loved the idea of magic. It made sense to me.

I should have loved the idea of Santa, except I can't remember a time I wasn't poor, and Santa doesn't visit poor kids.

December was my own personal hell. No winter solstice bonfire would ever be big enough to burn away all my anger at the forced cheer, demand for gifts, and unseasonable expectations.

I wasn't making New Year's Resolutions, I did that on my birthday in July.

I wasn't meeting anyone under the mistletoe, I wasn't that desperate.

I wasn't going to participate in the annual gift exchange, because somehow I always wound up with the bar of soap stolen from the pay-by-the-hour motel down the street.

I would be skipping the party, hitting the white sand beaches of Miami with a pink drink in hand, and spending my three days off catching up on N.W. Gehson's *Serial Killerz* series.

Maureen moved out from behind my desk and pouted. All of five-foot-nothing, she was a cute, apple-shaped woman with sunset pink hair and perpetually purple lips from a permanent makeup choice she made thirty years ago when she was twenty-one, drunk, and planning to be an exotic dancer all her life.[1]

In the bright blue sweater, she

---

[1] She still dances under the name Cotton Candy every other Friday down at the Sugar Strip on 4th, if you're wondering.

looked like the world's glummest Sugar Plum Fairy. She was holding a shiny blue paper with the words "All I Want For The Holidays" and a blank space for a holiday wish on it.

If I ignored the paper, I might escape further holiday interrogations.

"I... I was just trying to be nice!" A huge tear shimmered in her eye.

"I know." I patted her shoulder and tried very hard not to look at the tattoo peeking above her collar that HR insisted she keep covered during work hours. "But I don't like Christmas."

"This year is going to be different!" Maureen assured, her smile turning on like a floodlight in turtle season. "I figured out why you don't like Christmas."

"Because it's a commercial farce to celebrate capitalism?"

"No, silly! Because you're single! No one's giving you the good gifts." She winked and tried to bump me with her hip, but since her head only comes up to my shoulder even in kitten heels, it didn't quite work.

I scooted around her and into my three-sided box of an office.

There were sparkly confetti snowflakes covering the nameplate that had been a gift from one of my favorite metal-work artists.

Delinna Farmer was not a name that deserved to have snow on it. Especially fake snow.

Shaking the snow off the metal cut-out of my name, I smiled up at Maureen. "Really, Maureen, I'm fine."

"You will be!" She pulled a scroll of candy pink paper out of her cleavage so it unrolled in a long, curling list. "This is Auntie Maureen's list of acceptable bachelors in the greater Miami area."

"Maureen," I said, sitting down and giving her my very best glare, "if Rafael Kane is mentioned even once on that list, I will murder you. Right here and now. There will be blood all over your dancing elf sweater. No jury will convict me."

She rolled her eyes. "Tried that. Obviously there's chemistry there, but Rafe could have chemistry with a doorknob, so it doesn't matter." She put the list of names—written in pink and purple ink—on my desk. "Names. Numbers. Histories. Sizes."

"Siz—Oh!" I covered my mouth. "Sweet mother of pearl! Maureen! This is so invasive!" I crumpled the list up and dropped it in the recycling bin.

"A girl's got to know…"

"I do not need to know anyone's sizes!" I shouted as the door to the contracts office opened and the devil himself walked in.

Rafael's brown eyes went wide, his tan face frozen in a rictus of horror.

"I'm not participating in the company Christmas party and I'm not ordering the shirts," I said loudly, willing

Maureen to play along. Rafael might be the office grinch, but nobody gossiped as much as his people in the sales department. If he even guessed at the content of Maureen's list, I'd have every art gallery employee and intern in the greater Miami area sending me extra details.

Maureen, oblivious to the threat of Dick Pic Armageddon, crossed her arms over her ample chest. "Why not? What's wrong with the holiday party?"

"Because…" I scrambled for an excuse that wouldn't insult Maureen's party planning. "…I'm seeing someone."

Rafael snorted in amusement as he shook his head and walked to our copy machine by the door. The sales department had a better one, one that could print posters and banners, but it was broken and the sales associates had been bouncing in and out of the contracts office all week. There was nothing like the holidays to convince the obscenely wealthy to drop hundreds of thousands of dollars on art.

"Oh, sweetie," Maureen said, grabbing my arm and leaning in for a sideways hug as she ignored Rafael. "You don't need to lie."

"I'm not," I lied. "I am in a relationship. And I think it's serious. We are talking about moving in together."

From the copier Rafael gave me a look of disbelief that said, *No one would ever live with you.*

Maureen patted my hand with a tiny sigh of pity. "Let me guess. His name is Nick 'The Closer' Claus and you ordered him from the toys department at Lady Things downtown? I've met him too." Her smile was wicked. "But he doesn't count as a dinner date."

Too. Much. Information.

Closing my eyes, I focused on the filing list I needed to finish today. Anything to get the image of my middle-aged co-worker gleefully bouncing through the adult toy store out of my head.

In my imagination, she wore a frilled pink skirt that barely covered her ample thighs. I shuddered.

My only option was to lie more, or to hope Rafael would step in to help me. "Maureen—"

"No!" Rafael shouted from across the room. "No more. Not until I leave. I do not need to hear this. Let me finish. Please. Five more pages!"

Just for that I wanted to play dirty, but encouraging Maureen would give me a heart attack. There was only one course of action left…

"I'm getting a dog," I said before the dick pics became porno subscriptions in my stocking. "I've been visiting the shelters and I'm planning to adopt one over the holidays."

Maureen's shoulders sagged. "Honey, that does not count."

"A dog will be more loyal than any man will!" I drew myself up, a furious dark queen with a mask of rage perfected after years of studying every campy Halloween vampire movie ever. Morticia Addams, eat your heart out. "Probably more loyal than a woman, too. It'll love me, wait for me, and cuddle with me while I watch horror movies in December. A dog won't make me watch cheesy Christmas specials. A dog will go for walks on the beach with me. A dog will be happy eating whatever I cook—"

"A dog should have a high-protein diet."

Maureen and I both turned to stare.

Had Rafael Kane actually joined a conversation that wasn't about sales? After all these years?

"Do you like dogs?" Maureen asked politely, reverting back to Sweet Office Eccentric like a chameleon. "You've never mentioned them."

Rafael stared at the wall behind the copier as he realized his mistake. His body went rigid and I swear I saw a shiver of terror shimmy through him. He knew Maureen would never let him escape now.

"My mother raised dogs when I was growing up." He finished his copy work and turned to glare at me. "I've seen the stuff you eat for lunch, Del. Do the world a favor and stick to stuffed animals and battery-operated toys. A dog deserves better." He opened his mouth as if he were going to continue, then snapped it shut and marched out, back stiff.

Maureen hummed happily. "He has such a nice tush!"

"Maureen!" I smacked her arm.

"What? I'm married, not dead."

"We're at work."

"Quitting time was eight minutes ago. I can lust after people off the clock."

"You are a dirty old woman."

"Yes I am," she said proudly.

I rolled my eyes and remembered why I'd come back in. "I need to get my water bottles. I keep forgetting them." Nine of them sat in a row by my spare shoes.

"Oh, is that what happened?" Maureen asked. "I thought you'd decided to decorate with them. Maybe make a shrine to your beloved *agua*."

"Ha ha, funny." I grabbed a big bag with the name of a local farmer's stall on it and stuffed the water bottles inside. "The winter wonderland stuff. Can you keep it off my desk?"

Maureen pouted again.

"Please? I'll bring you some of those spiced pecans you like." If the bodega had a BOGO sale going on. If it wasn't buy-one-get-one, I wasn't sharing.

Her eyes went wide with delight. "Consider it gone. I will leave your corner a natural wasteland of bones, ghouls, and whatever that thing is," she said pointing to my Zany Zombie bobblehead.

"Thank you." I packed up and went home to research animal shelters. If I was going to be forced to participate in the holidays, I deserved to have someone who was happy to see me every day.

Surely I could get a dog for Christmas. It couldn't be that hard.

Keep reading! Head to
www.inkprintpress.com/lianabrooks/
christmas/werewolf/
to buy your copy now!

ABOUT THE AUTHOR

LIANA BROOKS is a summer child who loves hot days, sultry and humid nights, flowers growing wild, and the sound of summer rain. When she isn't swimming, she enjoys writing science fiction in every form, from sprawling space operas (*Fleet of Malik*) to the antics of a superhero family (*Heroes and Villains*).

You can learn more about her and her books at www.LianaBrooks.com

INKLETS

Collect them all! Released on the 1st and 15th of each month.

INKLET #055
Allure
AMY LAURENS

INKLET #056
The LIES We KNOW
LIANA BROOKS

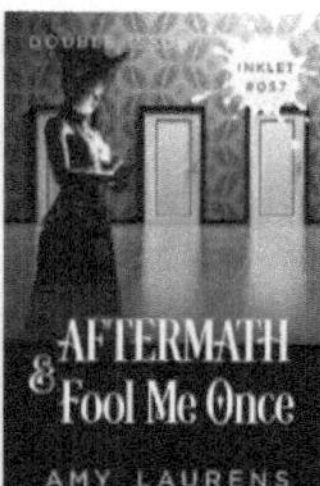
INKLET #057
AFTERMATH & Fool Me Once
AMY LAURENS

INKLET #058
Purity
An Age Of Unicorns Story
AMY LAURENS

INKLET #059
Saved
AMY LAURENS

INKLET #060
A Kiss is the Secret
AMY LAURENS

INKLET #061
A Changing Tides Story
Fire Bright
AMY LAURENS

INKLET #062
Hades AND Persephone
LIANA BROOKS

INKLET #063
Just So Long As You're Happy
AMY LAURENS

INKLET #064
Theft Of A Lifetime
LIANA BROOKS

INKLET #065
Shoe
AMY LAURENS

INKLET #066
Published AUTHOR
LIANA BROOKS

DOUBLE ISSUE
INKLET #067
THE REMARKABLE INSIGHT OF JELLYBEANS & Understanding
AMY LAURENS

INKLET #068
Desperate Measures
AMY LAURENS

INKLET #069
Rock-a-bye
LIANA BROOKS

INKLET #070
the Other Carly
AMY LAURENS

INKLET #071
Bs By Bioluminescent Light
AMY LAURENS

INKLET #072
Even Villains Grant Wishes
A Heroes & Villains Story
LIANA BROOKS

9 781925 825510